KB127537

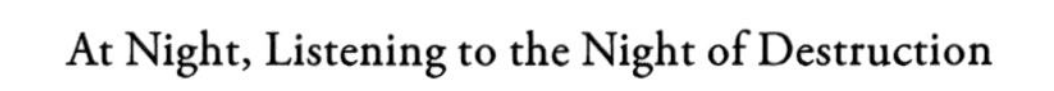
At Night, Listening to the Night of Destruction

At Night, Listening to the Night of Destruction

A collection of poems by Kim Myoung Ki

Translated by Jeon Seung-hee

멸망의 밤을 듣는 밤 김명기

K-Poet Series 039

ASIA

Contents

AT NIGHT, LISTENING TO THE NIGHT OF DESTRUCTION

Future Without a Future

Working on a sweltering hot midsummer day,
I bring my young colleagues a few cups of iced americanos.
Together with these youthful workers, who have just entered the minimum-hourly-wage market,
I drink coffee more expensive than our hourly rate.

Inside the coffee, as dark as the phrase "temporary worker,"
Are ice cubes, sparkling, and melting—
As an elder, who cannot tell them about hopes like those ice cubes, shamefully,

I try to save face with a few cups of ice coffee.

Even as they're feeling indignant about living
like this,
They have no choice but to live in this
servitude—I cannot be ignorant of that.
In order to live, even while mortgaging their
days endlessly,
They stand under the sizzling sun—I cannot
pretend not to know that.

So I share and drink my paltry wage with those
Who have recklessly joined in this life, being
ruthlessly cut down.

While listening helplessly and without paying
much attention to their fledgling stories
Of love, housing, and vague futures, stories that
will be broken again and again,
I cannot offer them even a cruel word of solace:
there is no ecstatic mercy in this world.

Although I am reminded of the heartless
summer days of
Surrenders older than me, who will someday no
longer be in this world,
Like the light-brown iced americanos showing
their bottoms, in order to shut my mouth,
Unable to talk about them, chewing lingering

ice cubes until my teeth freeze,
I think of the future, when even that
temporarily heroic past will no longer be.

Precariat*

Neo-liberalism divided even the proletariat into
classes.
Soviets that rose up with the Bolshevik
revolution, as if to build a new world,
Collapsed a long time ago.

On the day when the Soviet Union was
dissolved, an older friend of mine
Got drunk and cried as if the world had
collapsed—yet, a few years later,
He became a full-time professor, and now he is
living happily ever after as a tenured professor.

After graduating from a technical high school, a

friend of mine was hired at a steel company.
He lost his job during a national bankruptcy
and is now a construction worker,
Wandering all around the country.

Temporary workers at convenience stores who
endure darkness with their eyes open,
And Coupang friends who sell and mortgage
their bodies to conveyer belts,**
Revolving all night long for the sake of rocket
deliveries—Only after seeing them,
I realize that a "friend" is a cruel word, gnawing
at our lives day and night.

People who are closest to despair,
People who fill spaces left empty by death, just
to eat,
Death by being trapped, death by falling, death
by being dragged, death while walking.

The last and tiniest component of evolving
capitalism that degrades
Workers: their hourly wage as their class, as they
move from one bottom
To another, while ever lowering their bodies
behind unfamiliar desires and betrayed
expectations—

The hourly wage that cannot be split further
dropped before the threshold called
minimum,
And did not go over $8 this year. And, as if
urging slavish labor, like debt,
The employment contract, printed like a last-
call notice, clarifies to the trivial employee:

Employment type: short-term temporary worker
Hourly wage: 2024 minimum hourly wage
($7.80)

* Precariat is a group of temporary laborers who are not given job security and who receive low wages.

** [Translator's Note] Coupang is an online retailer in South Korea that is similar to Amazon. "Coupang friends" is a term used for their employees.

Evening News*

Like a baseball flying toward cheering bleachers,
Missiles fly above a moaning people.
While a batter is running toward home, led by
  tanks,
Ground forces are racing toward ruins. When a
  baby
In the arms of his cheering dad smiles brightly
  with open arms,
A baby in the arms of his shrieking mom
Is dying while bleeding. In the baseball field, to
  brighten the darkness,
The lights are turned on, while over the ruins, as
  if to hasten death,
Flares flash. While in the baseball field roaring

cheers
Reverberate, mastic trees of a foreign country in
flames
Are shuddering. The longer traces are made by
humans in the air,
The bigger desires and fears grow—and home
runs and the homeless
Fly together into the roofless air.
One might wonder how this can be
In front of people who are rushed to death,
With black faces and without wills,
But how can we feign ignorance about
The fact that these anonymous deaths, popping
up like old phlegm,

Were once lives cheering?
While people stop cheering and return home,
While chief mourners unable to wear mourning
clothes are crying
In front of destroyed houses, between chilled
desires and delayed
Fears, finally, the air becomes an empty space,
And, like closed eyes of premature babies in
incubators
Who died as soon as they were born, darkness
descends—
And a man with a bloody bandage around his
head, over the ruins,
Toward God's grace gotten lost on its way,

Kneels down and slowly raises his arms.

* On November 13, 2023, the LG baseball team won the first Korean Series title in 29 years. On the same day, Israel attacked hospitals and schools in Gaza, sheltering civilian refugees, killing and injuring hundreds of Palestinians. As the electricity in hospitals was cut off, victims included premature babies in incubators. It is estimated that about half of the more than 10,000 civilians massacred lately were children, including premature babies.

Discarding Shoes

I discard the shoes I have worn for more than
ten years.
Their heels got bent like the small of my back,
As they had to bear the weight of my body as it
moved at its will;
And there are wounds torn and dug wide and
deep on them.
Although I changed soles and patched linings
Again and again, as if renewing a contract,
As they were supporting the body of a
temporary worker's life,
From under the soles agape like holes, as if
saying they couldn't stand it anymore,
Drooping socks pushed through

Like old tongues.
Although how my life had been, while one
   bottom was pushing another,
Was fully revealed, my embarrassment,
Rather than sadness, was like mail returned to
   the sender,
As it got lost and became dirtier.
What could be more miserable
Than the pitiable that cannot be condemned?
A corner of my life, crippled
At the end of darkness, as it was vomiting
Even the nastiest stench hidden deep inside
During its life enduring damp shades,
Must now wander around the world as an

unknown sender.
I am now discarding my shoes. While hiding
traces of cruelty by cleaning them
And sealing off an envelope without a postmark
To make sure that they won't come back, so that
they
Will never meet the bottom again, I take my
feet out of them and throw them away.

Edith Piaf*

Please don't! You do know this world is not as beautiful as your song, don't you? How wretched a song must have been that a battered young prostitute sang like a little bird! I cannot understand even a measure of your song. But how could I not know the sorrow hidden in your voice? There are things that stand out, the more you try to hide. Like you who said you'd choose love over your country, people who disregard humiliation and shame to survive no longer sing. When occasionally I feel pity for your wet heart, I browse through your forgotten songs, but there is no way they'll revive a brilliant life. Sometimes, I think that people live until they die just because. I know of Paris, the Eiffel Tower, Louvre Museum, the Mirabeau Bridge that Guillaume Apollinaire** is supposed to have crossed, and the Basilica of Sacre Coeur de Montmartre, where Picasso went for a mass during his exile, but how futile! I have never been to France. Living is like that, I suppose. Although you know a lot of things, they are mostly useless. As I know your song that I cannot understand is a *chanson*, people know and don't know things at the same time. Children, who learned early on that *la vie en rose* is not for them, just grow old while living like thorns on a rose. Although I know that pleasure and collapse are heteronyms, today I saw a young death that collapsed without growing old. A 17-year-old boy of Algerian descent, a country that used to be a French colony—if this boy of the same age as you when you were selling your body and gave birth to your first daughter—if his skin were white, would he have been shot? A non-white man, I have no plan to visit France even in the future. When I hear your song coming from somewhere, I'll just think that I am living just because, listening to your anthem like a dirge, *padam, padam, padam...*

* Edith Piaf (1915-1963) was the French singer known as “the little sparrow.” She is considered the best post-World War II singer in France.

** Guillaume Apollinaire (1880-1918) was a French poet, writer, critic, and art theorist. He tried to introduce calligramme into sentences and is considered a pioneer of surrealism.

Landlord

It has been 11 years since Father passed away.
When he died, Mother inherited his legacy.
After 11 years, just like that, out of the blue,
A piece of land owned by Father appeared.

Father, who became a mountain supervisor after
death, was on paper
Landlord of a patch of land. In order to inherit
a right to a 1,300-square-meter slope,
Not worth even a three-square-meter plot in
Gangnam, I had
To obtain various documents.

For my right of possession, all the previous

owners
Were summoned through family registration
certificates.
From the certificates of Father and Grandfather,
I found that the owner of this land before
Father was not Grandfather.

The name of a stranger, who was declared dead
after a period of being missing—
What I found was the name of my father's
elder brother about whom I had heard only
vaguely.
The name everyone avoided,
Because he chose the North as his fatherland,

Popped up out of the blue—like the land.

Uncle, who must have been a dead person even
when he was alive—
Preceded by this blood relative of mine who
deserted the world,
From our lonely pedigree, a right to the land
reached me.

Like names that have undergone the colonial
period and endless ideological strife,
An angular and steep land with which I know
neither what to do
Nor how long it was unused—

I became its landlord.

At Night, Listening to Night of Destruction*

At night I listen to Hahn Dae-soo's Night of
Destruction—
His rough sound of breathing like the sound of
cutting steel and his controlled husky voice
Resemble primitive art, like cave murals and
petroglyphs.
People who were dying while scratching the
walls of Bangudae or the Cave of Altamira
Must have died when they were getting used to
the pains of hard labor.**
They must have killed whales carrying their
young,
Killed buffalos embracing their calves—killed
them

To live. While they were accumulating
slaughtered bodies,
Humans were hiding their guilty feelings deep
inside their genes,
And evolved into bodies killing to take.
One day, when someone for the first time killed
another person,
Did he know that his blood-soaked hand was
The ancient future? Did he know that the body
that killed to live
Would end up living to kill? On the day the
Berlin Wall fell,
People cheered in front of the Brandenburg
Gate,

Thinking there would be no more wars,
And passionately embraced one another, as if
they were the hope of humanity.
But before the 20th century was over, many
missiles
Flew through the night sky over the Gulf, like
fireworks,
And airplanes hit the Twin Towers in New York
As soon as the 21st century began: They were
specters of *homo sapiens sapiens*,
Like Abel of the *Old Testament*, the first
murderer of a human.
The night when tiny feet inside the incubators
in Al Shifa Hospital in Gaza

Died without even knowing they were born,
Like tiny notes written on a score never to be
heard—
The night of destruction that is irredeemable
Will come like that, burying greed that does not
know humiliation
And eternal sadness into a bottomless pit,
Like the desperate voice of an old singer who
does not sing about the future.

* “Night of Destruction” is the fifth song in singer-song-writer Hahn Dae-soo’s fifth album, *Eternal Sorrow*.

** [Translator’s Note] The Bangudae Petroglyphs are prehistoric engravings on flat, vertical rock faces, located in Ulsan, South Korea; The Cave of Altamira is a cave complex located near the historic town of Santillana del Mar in Cantabria, Spain. It is renowned for its prehistoric cave art featuring charcoal drawings and polychrome paintings of local fauna and human hands.

Himalayan *Haeguk* (Sea Chrysanthemum)

Haeguk blooms around the time when all the
other flowers fall.
They are flowers remaining last along the seaside
slope.
I hear that it already snowed in some mountain
regions,
But it rains endlessly here on the flowers on a
precarious slope.

When carrying loads many times bigger than
his body,
And climbing Himalayan slopes while wearing
sandals,
A boy blinks his bright eyes,

Father, who had four frost-bitten toes
  amputated,
Hobbles around the snow-covered yard
In search for a bottle his wife hid.

When the sick father, who handed down only
  nasty slopes to his son,
Drops tears over a liquor glass;
Between the young eyes barely managing to
  climb a steep valley
And the frayed sandals patched many times
  over,

Like footprints left behind by cracked heels,

While *haeguk* is spreading from one shady slope
to another,
Into the world embracing life from which there
is no escape,
Shiftlessly it rains, it snows.

White-Haired Madman

A man sending incantations on a wind for days
After hanging a tattered bedsheet near the sea
Like a *rongda* or a *tharchog* that has fluttered for
a long time on the Tibet Plateau*
No matter how carefully you listen, it is
impossible to understand his words.
He could be calling his own soul that left his
body
And went over to the other world, or he might
be desperately
Looking for someone who has not returned
from the sea.
Yet his words, scattered over the waves, are
buried under the foam

And vanish without leaving any traces.
We all have moments when we want to talk to
ourselves,
Like when we desperately miss someone whom
we can see never again,
Or when it seems that the whole world is
collapsing, as we scold ourselves
For being careless, as our lives seem to touch the
polar region.
Where have all the ardent desires gone, which
seeped out of our bones?
Without stretching his bent back, standing on a
spot, unconcerned,
The man is beseeching desperately; as if sending

away even last night's nightmares,
Infinitely light is the sheet fluttering.

* A *rongda* is five-colored cloth on which Tibetan Buddhist scriptures are written. It is hung on a long pole. A *tharchog* is the same five-colored cloth hung on a long string.

Cutting a Donarium Cherry

Father planted the seedling of a donarium
cherry, thin like a shovel handle
After building our house near the brook at the
foot of a mountain.
While it was growing thicker than a thigh,
Beautiful flowers bloomed in spring, like pink
wads of cotton.

Although the tree grew sturdily for more than
20 years,
Branches grown thicker together with such a
body
Knocked at our roof on a windy day,
Or scratched our windows. As this tree with

beautiful flowers
Grew, our concerns were growing, too.

While looking up at the tree, whose leaves grew
as big as our palms,
As flowers fell and the sap rose, we decided to
cut it
In its hard middle above the roof.
As I tried to push the sawblade, standing on a
ladder,
Its life, solidified during its struggle for life,
Did not allow it to open its node easily.

While forcing the sawblade into the tree, biting

and withstanding the blade
In order not to be broken, I thought of the
days when I endured disquietudes and
misfortunes,
Like the sawblade. Whether a tree or a human,
it is not easy
To break them at their height.

To chop the cut tree into pieces,
I dried it for days in the shade. Losing sap, it
Gradually dried and its leaves withered.
Finally, the wood obediently accepted the
sawblade.
For a life to set is to become gentler,

After tenaciously enduring and withstanding. At
some point, for me, too,
A day will come when I accept the last sawblade.

While I Am Thinking Of These Things

On my way from Gyeongpo along the coastal trail
To Jumunjin, on the sliding door of an old inn,
At the Sungeut Beach past Sageunjin,
A discolored sign reading "Monthly Rental Available"
Is swinging. People without key money
Push this old sign away and enter the room to rest.
Although they say that we all rent this world briefly,
To rent a room at a damp place where the ocean fog
Seeps under the floor paper in early morning is

to briefly lay an empty body
So that it might communicate with black
fungi. For a person who can get up and leave
anytime
For the work of living, his body is the bedding,
furniture, and dishes.
Where else in this world would there be such a
light, moving load?
As I am thinking of
The days when I felt like leaving this world, in a
tiny room
Without sunlight, the time when I was bruised
from hunger and poverty
While hanging around the dwellings of

wanderers,
As if folding a directionless life and throwing it
into the corner of a room—
While I am thinking of these things,
A person who hasn't yet arrived at the swinging
sign
Might be managing to drag his body, his only
possession,
And pass a point in this world like an exile.

High-Sea Watch

All day long, gusty winds, and a high-sea watch was issued on the sea. Although ships of unknown sizes passed occasionally along the horizon, there was no ship going out to sea gushing spray or returning to the port leading seagulls. Watching waves roughly pushed and wrecked like furrows meeting one another in an old slash-and-burn field, I thought of the first wave about to be born inside the bosom of the winds.

On my way to lunch, I saw a man drunk from daytime drinking leaning precariously on a wall and wailing. As if I found something I'd lost, I forgot my lunch and stood there, watching him for a long time. The wall on which he barely managed to lean was listening to his struggle that everyone must experience a few times in life, and his sorrowful variations that moved his body up and down, because of his lingering feelings, regrets, and remorse that nobody could console.

On a late summer afternoon, when even cicadas' shrill, soul-carving chirruping quieted down, Bob Dylan's voice sang in my earphones, "The answer…is blowin' in the wind." But could the wind, joined together with the rough waves, know genuine life and everlasting peace? Living a life while forgetting others' sorrows too easily and mine, too, I am a person already addicted to pain, one who recognizes a painful wailing only when he sees it, like a weathervane that turns only when it is hit by the wind.

As the sun set and the wind's inside story was still vague, the man either stopped crying or was quietly sobbing. And while I was wondering when I last wailed and when my next wailing, that would move my body up and down, would come, the day set at the workplace over the sea. A day like this had always been there and will always be, too. As Bedouins, known for their inability to be united like sands, ironically lasted for thousands of years while wandering in the deserts, so after leaving the high-sea watch and wailing, like other people, at the wasteland, as if to move my life to another dwelling, I hurried to leave work.

Corpse

With a younger brother suffering from a brain
disease, he lived
In a remote hilltop. He neither farmed,
Nor worked as a day laborer. The small benefits
his brother received
And falling down whenever he was even
brushed by someone
With whom he picked a fight were his only
livelihood.
His neighbors had long ago given up on him.
One early summer evening, he obstructed my
car
In front of his house, on my way back from
work.

When I asked him angrily what the matter was,
he said, calmly,
With his hands clasped behind his back, that
because I often
Passed by his house and raised dust, I should
pay him
Two hundred dollars. From his mouth, a smell
of hard liquor
Wafted. After that demand, he deftly raised his
body, so tiny
Because he had led such a life for more than 60
years,
And pushed it, as if throwing, into the backyard
of his house. He looked

Like a small and empty pot. Although I
expected a call from him during dinner,
And all kinds of curses, together with mentions
of medical certificates,
Nothing happened.
On the third evening, I heard the news
That his body, like a thin pot, had been broken;
That he had just sent his disabled brother to a
facility. If I had given him $200 that day,
Would he have held onto his cracked life a little
longer and managed to stay on?
Sending $200 to the corpse, after the autopsy,
I thought of his extremely thin body. The smell
of hard liquor

Wafting in the still-hot evening sun from a
person
With whom I had not had a decent
conversation—
It might have been his last sincerity. Yet I turned
it down,
And, when I heard the news that he was
shattered, I stroked my chest.
Feeling as if I turned away from a moment that
I did not know,
The moment when he might have been living
fully, no matter how paltry a life,
I avoid that hilltop, where there is no longer any
trace of human presence,

And return home a roundabout way along the
brook for days.

While Quietly Pushing Away Sadness

Into the darkness during a cold snap, people
Hurried and scattered, and he was crying.
At the corner of the eaves of a funeral hall,
  amidst snow flurries
Like prematurely gray hair, with sadness
That was neither wailing nor a hushed sobbing
  filling his eyelids,
As if pushing away words of condolence that
  were of no help,
He was sending away regrets, little by little.
In front of the ash-filled incense burner and the
  portrait of the deceased,
He exchanged bows with mourners and calmly
  offered them hot meals,

Without making a crying sound.
While the body free of life was cooling down,
Although people shared stories of their lives
until then, and to come,
While putting rice into *yukgaejang* soup, they
could not
Talk about the deceased,
After whom they could no longer inquire. In a
low voice,
Someone said hasty words of pity: It was better
this way,
As he had been oppressed with worries taking
care of his sick family for a long time,
And nodded as if seeking agreement.

As we cannot figure out the mind of a person
Who took care of the patient, and who was
even more precarious than him,
What can we say about his mind wanting to
hold onto the patient even a little longer?
On a harsh night when the news of severe
winter snow crosses
The subtitles on the muted TV screen, like
sealed lips,
Darkness is deepening while burying light.
Although there seems a night of paradise that
will
Accept the body from which the sense of pain
disappeared,

Wreaths of condolence are diligently looking for
the dead far into the night,
As if urging us to hold onto life until the very
last moment.
While he was quietly pushing away sadness
alone,
The living turned their backs from the person
who would never return,
And did not refuse a hot meal for the days when
they should continue to live.

Heartbroken in Spring

Someone asked me how not to have one's heart broken. How would I know such a thing? As our heart is like a flower, it stays fallen far longer than in bloom, how can we deny that? There are days when we are reminded of an incident for a long time. Like residual images growing as time goes by, the moment when nothing, like a walk on a spring day, becomes something, I am already a person whose heart has been broken numerous times. If I was asked how to have one's heart broken, I perhaps would have talked about such a spring day. At a question that I cannot answer, unable to say a word, I alternate my gaze between falling magnolias and blooming cherries. There are so many hearts about to fall along the river, and I would not have lived like this, if I could. I could not have lived like this.

Monsoon

Although I knew that frequent mistrust of someone one trusted was unhappiness, time flew helplessly. Although I have lived from the spring to the fall placidly, they were in fact depressing days. Although I knew that my life's place to which I could never return was passing by, while I was walking alone, eating alone, and doing something alone, I wasn't too sad. Then, the winter came, but I was still alone, like a person who never gets tired. Understanding untrustworthy times as if I understood expressionless faces of people behind masks, I got on the plane to a faraway country where it was supposed to rain frequently.

In a strange February, to which I arrived after hours of flying, I walked, hunched from gout, when I ran into a rain shower like a good-bye. Finding shelter under the eaves in a foreign country, I thought of the days when my heart was infinitely drenched. When I saw ends everywhere as living felt like a remote island, I wanted to move from one end to the other of a wind and spread myself out in both rainy and dry seasons. There was no difference between being wet and being dry. After suffering alone for days because I could not look away from things, although I tried hard to look away, I found several days had disappeared.

I did not say anything to my heart that had worked so hard to come here while following the body that wanted to become something but could not become anything. As the words I had thought for a long time had already become yearning, it did not matter whether they were fulfilled or not. Although I dried my wet body until dark, my wet heart was not consoled at all, even by moving residence. Although it rained overnight, as if to wash me, who had fallen asleep after yearning for sadness that did not brush against me or that simply passed me by, the tops of my feet, swollen from gout, did not easily subside, just like my mistrust that could not be erased.

When Sadness Gathers Between the Sound of Rain and the Sound of Breathing

In the fall when I was 25, my paternal grandmother, who had lived 85 years, passed away. Five years later, my maternal grandmother, who had suffered from a chronic disease, took her last, difficult breath. Leaves fallen from a persimmon tree covered the backyard. It was the end of my grandparents' generation. The death of my father, who lived like fire all his life, came similarly. Twelve years ago, he suddenly threw away the nameplate of his life into the concrete pipe near the brook. It was November. A few months later, his sister, my third paternal aunt, and his cousin, my paternal first cousin once removed, followed him into death.

On a day when a September typhoon surged, my other, elder paternal first cousin once removed let go of his life. The funeral in the rain was dignified. Surrounding the grave, dug beforehand in the rain, the Seventh Day Adventists sang hymns and held a service, while my elderly mother crossed herself toward her husband's cousin's casket. His second cousins, elderly ladies, dropped tears over the raindrops. All things felt vacant. His widow, who had lost her mind long before then, continued to sleep in the funereal bus, without wearing a mourning dress. Mother, Aunt, and two Uncles, gradually leaving this world, were precariously supporting the generation above me. Shrunk like the crescent moon, elderlies, already over or nearing 80, bowed toward life's last chapter.

The storm was growing more furious, and I had nothing more to do than supporting my mother, but I felt as if I should be doing something more. Back home, my body still wet, a cigarette between my teeth, flipping through a few books of poetry, I thought of people who died in the fall. Dried leaves of a cherry tree holding rainwater bumped against the window and fell. The paltry leaves still holding on endured the night of a typhoon like my parents' generation now barely managing to stand. Like sadness gathering between the sound of rain and the sound of breathing.

The Year Zero, in Winter

Father passed away suddenly, under a persimmon tree, in the early fall, without leaving a will. His legacies were two abandoned dogs, a battered car, and a wooden house he built himself. Twelve years ago, I rushed back home because of his death. The battered car stopped a month later, perhaps because it could not accept its new owner. The dogs that had been following his heels endured only a few more exhausted years, until they followed him. Only the house, with the stream along its backyard, remains, and has become a body encircling my old mother and me growing old.

Father left the house he built, after living there for 10 years, and I have lived in it for 12 years after returning to it. After 22 years, the wooden house requires more care every year. I added a deck and a sunroom and apply oil every three years. Although this shabby house, holding out, while swallowing money like a bed-ridden patient, for 12 years, is a legacy of my discord with Father, with whom I could never reconcile, both Mother and I know this is the last stop of our lives, as it was for Father's.

Although I think of things that disappeared, and things that will disappear, while listening to the moaning of my elderly mother suffering from pain in her body for a few days, and the creaking of twisted rafters of an old house trying to straighten themselves, only the things that cannot be named traverse my life, as I haven't given my heart to anywhere. This winter, full of a main body without a preface, will also not acquire any name; only the sound of breaths, shortened while leaning on the shortened sun-rays, is managing to add a single sentence.

At night, when cats leave footprints along the edge of a yard, where lingering snow flurries swirl along with the winds, the spring is faraway, and the lives out in the cold hover around in pursuit of human presence, in search for a place to warm their bodies. As they also have sorrows, they occasionally squat after drinking water from the stream, where thin ice sheets are floating, and make indistinct low cries. Then, abandoned dogs admitted into my house bark loudly, perhaps in sympathy with the sorrows outside, which they must have experienced before.

Land's End

Winds, having lost their way, move from one
tree to another.
Perhaps because they also know that this is their
end?
Like an exile driven out from an unbearable
time,
Like flocks of birds flying north over the sea
All day long, they suffer from homesickness.
Half of the business of living is to sigh, and the
rest is
To moan. Although contours appear
Like weaknesses that have been hidden
At the end of the end that has become longer,
As the sea goes out while pushing away its body,

how could I not know
That it is more shameful to hide what is
shameful than not to hide it?
As I am sad that I forgive myself,
As I grow older and become more shameless,
I now cannot even try to make a pledge to
myself.
While I am wavering, like the word that cannot
find its way to the next one
In a word-chain game, winds have left for
another road.
Cooling down its body, while shedding leaves
over the sea,
A tree insists on pulling its empty shadow

toward the area below its ankle.

Vast and faraway, this is

The outside of the outside.

The Work of Living

In the early spring, a forest fire erupted. For 11
days
Even forests faraway burned to the ground.
After the trees had burned, though,
The mountains remained as they were, but like
blackened furnaces.
Water deer, racoons, and wild pigs, avoiding the
fire,
Ran down even to the main street. But as they
had nowhere else to go,
They reluctantly returned to the charred remains
of the mountain forests.
Humans who had lost their houses to the fire,
like the helpless

Mountain animals, also had nowhere else to go,
So they brought containers like huts to live in
At the foothills of the mountains.

POET'S NOTE

Kittens asking for food in front of the porch at dusk fall asleep under the *thoenmaru* wooden porch. Looking carefully, you can see them licking around their mouths with tiny tongues. Perhaps they are dreaming. All living beings move somehow. Life is precious not only for us humans. Sometimes, abandoned dogs find their way here, and cats born wild live together in my house. There is nothing more that a human being can do than offer food and water to these lives. Although I don't know how or why they end up here, there is nothing else a living being can do than to take care of the living.

Living life is a work of living while bearing the existence of a hidden side. Watching lives struggling alone, to survive even in deprivation, unhappiness, and inconvenient absurdities, I find them sad, pitiful, and lonesome. On winter nights, the hushed cries of those lives endure a long and thick darkness together. Is poetry different? While gathering poems to publish them, I always feel like I'm collecting new instances of unhappiness. Managing just barely to hold onto a time of ordeals, when one feels discarded, collapsing, and dismantled, I hold out. This collection of poems is also a record of an unhappiness with unknown directions. It contains prayers of *please* and tragedies of *at last*. What else could I do?

— Kim Myoung Ki, at his shabby house in a remote village on the threshold of spring 2024

POET'S ESSAY

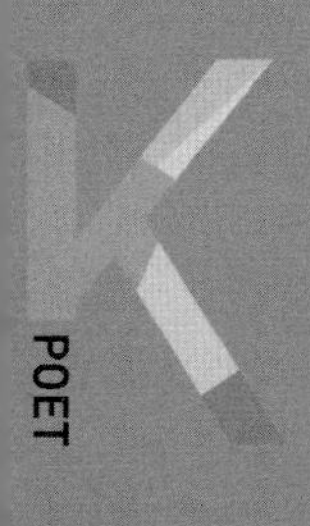

Living at the Crossroads of the Twelve Passes

The Village

The living somehow manage to keep on living. The village where I live is in a remote mountain area about 20 kilometers from town and village centers. It's a village formed naturally as people gathered there for a long time. Although there's no knowing exactly how long it has existed, it must have been around at least 300 years, as there is a grave of my ancestor seven generations back, where my placenta was buried. Its formal administrative name is Ducheon-ri, Buk-myeon, Uljin-gun, Gyeongsangbuk-do. Although we sometimes divide it into Oeducheon and

Naeducheon, with Ducheon Stream in the middle, we also call it by its nickname, Mallae. So Ducheon is its administrative name and Mallae is its original name that villagers have long used for it. Mallae is also divided into Anmallae and Bakkatmallae on each side of the same stream. Although there are 16 households in Anmallae and about 20 in Bakkatmallae, the total population of the village is fewer than 50 people, because many houses have remained empty for a long time. It has been a long time since scenes disappeared, such as villagers playing the *yunnori* board game during holidays and children walking to school along the stream.

My house is the last one on a hilltop in Anmallae. A valley named Keungol begins here. When you look down from our yard, you can see the entire village. While looking down, I occasionally wonder about the lifespan of this village. You can find gradually more assisting walkers and canes in the Village Assembly Hall, where people used to play the *yunnori* board game, while shabby tractors and battered cars pass by slowly. As if looking at the transparent innards of a drying fish, I can see the village drying out, while exposing its insides. At just above the age of 50, the age Confucius said to be that of knowing the Heavenly Mandate, I am lowering the average age of the village. Nevertheless, there are no idle fields in this village. As villagers have been holding onto their lands, which have never increased, they calmly cultivate the fields, as if doing so is a custom or inertia. Although my placenta is buried here, I have wandered other places since childhood. I went to schools and worked at places unrelated to this village. Whenever I dropped by or passed it, I was busy turning around and leaving it. When my stubborn father collapsed and passed away, I was very far away. That was in early winter 12 years ago. I came here then to take care of his funeral and did not return to the city. Now I have been living for 12 years in this home village, where I had neither lived nor do I pretend to farm.

Around two years after I returned to this village, a palatial, tile-roofed building began to go up in the middle of it. This was followed by the construction of many other structures around it. It was called the Project of Restoring the Tavern District in Sibiryeong (the Twelve Passes). There had been a tavern street in this village a long time ago; it was where peddlers, traveling back and forth, between Heungbu Fair on the beach and Chunyang Fair inland, satisfied their hunger and thirst and took naps. Although inns at that time would not have been palatial, the restoration project was centered on this grand house. It was a typical bureaucratic project, set off with the word "restoration." Villagers were excited and expectant, and I also briefly wondered if it might lengthen the lifespan of this village declining toward extinction. But I did not expect much. I have yet to see a successful example of a governmental restoration project, which was in vogue for a while. The tavern district that they claimed to be a project that would benefit villagers, completed after years of construction, but did not benefit the villagers. It stood alone and barely managed to operate with a consignment agent. The village surrounding it has been continuing its decline, like sunlight in late fall.

Yet this story is neither tragic nor ill-fated. The living will somehow manage to live, and a natural village will return to nature, once its lifespan is over. It will return to its origin. Although cities are growing bigger and more complex by the day, small villages are still their background. Children who went to school along the sides of streams and ears of yellowing rice filling fields were the foundation for the cities gradually prospering more and more. Although we often hear about people returning to the countryside or villages, they are mostly people retiring. We probably won't return to the time when this village was hustling and bustling. Still, I hope we don't forget that humans are connected with one another. Even the skyscrapers, feeding on the shades of crafty villages, began in fields 20 kilometers away from towns and village centers. Life is not always defined by clarity. It is just the things happening during our lives. No matter where a place is, it will someday be extinct and return to an origin. The village is just openhandedly accepting its fate in time and space.

The People

As in most villages, people here work continuously. I do not farm professionally, but instead go to nearby towns and villages for work. My elderly mother spends her days doing light jobs specifically designed for seniors, while taking care of our vegetable gardens, or brushing and cleaning up our backyard. During my childhood, as I remember, most people farmed to feed themselves. As the first son in my family and clan, I was sent to a city when I was young. While my cousins ten years younger held up the guide lines for rice planting, helped with threshing, cut grass for cows and bulls, and carried loads on their backs, I visited home only briefly during vacation times and ate white rice that Grandmother specially cooked for me, instead of the dark-colored barley that my younger cousins ate. As a child, I was told that was how it should be. Uncles and aunts did not complain about it. Not only my cousins but also my peers and friends lived similar lives. They worked like sturdy young men about the time when they entered middle school. At some point, however, all those cousins and friends went to the cities, and I returned home relatively younger than the others.

Some of my vigorous relatives are no longer in this world. Even my father, who seemed like he would live easily to a hundred, took down his life's signpost at 74. Fathers of my friends and my father's friends are also sick or barely managing to work with frail bodies. Although we live in a time when food is abundant, the villagers live the same way as when they had to farm to live. While older people who looked incredibly sturdy are no longer around or became frail elderlies, all the children grew up and left.

People keep moving their bodies to feed them. Plants holding onto their exhaustion grow upright under the summer's heat. Most people living here were born and raised, and formed families here. The place where they have lived with all their might is a tiny village smaller than four by four kilometers. Here, it seems that only people, not the world, change. If the world has changed, they should be enjoying prosperity and health; but they work in the fields that do not grow larger with their bent backs and sick bodies, until just before they die. Then they are buried on the hills behind the village—and that is the end of their lives. Although I sometimes hear complaints about such an existence, it cannot be a wrong life. There are quite a few axes and hoes with glossy smooth handles in every house, and there are mountainous piles of firewood in some houses.

Although their arms, like cast iron, have become thinner, and their backs, like a large cauldron lid, have shrunk, and although their calves with thick sinews have disappeared, they have never deviated from their lives. Who could dare to call that a stuffy, foolish existence? Cities have grown bigger and more complex and convenient, as much as the villagers have shed sweat and their bodies have shrunk. For life, any place where it stands is the center. Therefore, the center of people remaining here is this village, smaller than a few square kilometers, and someday they will put down all things and finish their lives.

The Road

The main street ends at the village. There are two roads coming toward the village from nearby towns. Now paved, clean, and wide, 20 years ago they were narrow and unpaved dirt roads. When it rained or snowed, the bus that stopped at the village only three times a day would often not come. My grandparents and their ancestors walked a narrow and rugged 20-kilometer lane to a nearby town all their lives. Father and mother walked for half of their lives, while I always used buses or cars, except for a brief early period that I don't remember. Before then, when peddlers came and went, they must have walked along the trails at the foot of the hills, over narrow ridges between paddies, and across streams and brooks.

The name of the village, Mallae, means a place that comes last. I commute on a road, where cherry blossoms appear like a tunnel in the spring, and common zinnias bloom between summer and fall. It takes only about 20 minutes by car to get to nearby towns. Once people walked all day to cover the distance that now takes less than an hour. Their bundles were almost always small. They often took wild plants or herbs to the fair; millet, sorghum, beans and red beans after the fall harvest; and firewood many times the size of their bodies on their backs in winter, when there was nothing else to sell. This was what they did to survive. For survival, there would have been no reason not to take the roads, no matter how hard it might have been, but that did not always happen.

My uncle, my father's unmarried elder brother, went to the North through those roads. He was considered missing, then officially dead. My aunt, my father's elder sister, took the roads with only a single bundle, to be married, as if driven out. My family lost contact with her, and now we don't know whether she is alive or dead. I have never seen their faces. Father and uncle took those roads to go to the battlefields in another country, and barely managed to survive and return. As life and death repeated themselves, the roads became gradually wider and better. One day, outsiders poured in on those roads. The Twelve Passes Road which peddlers used to take was named the Geumgangsong Supgil, or Red Pine Forest Trail. The hills behind the village became healing forest paths. The pass, where peddlers would take back-carriers full of crops to exchange them for dried fish, seaweed, and salt, was crowded with colorful tourists. Bed and Breakfasts sprouted up in the village and the palatial tile-roofed Peddlers Tavern District was built. People who wanted to do a walk on narrow and rugged roads gathered from all over the country, using the roads that had become wide and smooth, while being born and dying again and again.

The spacious parking lot newly built at the end of the main street was filled with sedans and tourist buses carrying outsiders. Our village, on its way toward declining, seemed to regain life from them. People appeared everywhere in the village, taking pictures and greeting villagers. It did not look bad for the residents. But the liveliness did not last long, like a tonic with a momentary effect. Similar roads sprouted up all over the country, in both cities and villages. People began searching out newer roads, and gradually fewer arrived on the narrow roads.

I realized then that a road has the structure appropriate for its use. I have walked the Twelve Passes Road from Ducheon to Sogwang-ri near Chunyang a couple of times. Except for the paths built to carry woods, here and there, it was a narrow road on which barely two or three people could walk side-by-side. I could understand why porters in the old days rested standing rather than sitting down—there was no place to sit.

The *bajige* carrier they used is a carrier on which they put a *balchae* basket made of bush clovers or bamboo strips in order to maximize the space for loads. On that slope, they must not have been even able to consider taking down and reloading such a heavy load. What they needed was not a wider road—but a shortcut. In order not to take a roundabout way but a shortcut, they had to take a narrow and steep path. That kind of road did not damage the forests full of large pine trees.

Although it was a road for survival for some in the old days, a few hundred years later, it became a road for healing those exhausted from survival. Still, visitors to the road gradually decreased and the villagers' brief and lively expectation subsided. Although there are still visitors from time to time, who are looking for a quiet forest path, the road is still there just as a road. Like a village or a people, the road will someday return to its beginning, when its role is over, and become a dense green, primitive forest. All are in harmony, yet all are also distinct.

The House

The house is quiet all day. Except for a postman or a delivery truck occasionally arriving, there is no sound of a human presence. There are only the sounds of Northern bamboo brushing against one another on the hills behind my house and that of streams along the margin of my backyard. A rather large typhoon is heading north along the eastern coast. After a particularly long, rainy season is over, we are now anticipating a few days of rain. I once heard that a typhoon represents the tears gathered from sad people and poured over a place. If that is true, how many sad people are there in this world? It has been 12 years since I returned to this home below the pass. Meanwhile, I have lived a trivial life, and I will continue to do so.

I like the broad meaning of the word "life"—a word colorful, simple, complex, and singular. Although I returned home, the necessity of my return is not outside of the purview of this universal word life. What difference would there be between living under a pass and living at a faraway place? There are either those who know here or those who don't know, and either those who have been here or those who haven't. At the end of the summer, when winds change, I am waiting for the typhoon approaching now.

COMMENTARY

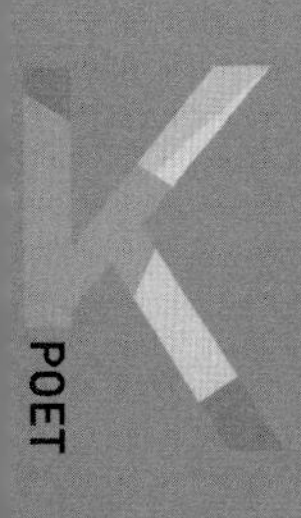

Hope Like Sparkling, Melting Ice Cubes

Yoo Sungho (Literary Critic)

Kim Myoung Ki's poems show exceptional strengths within the contemporary Korean poetic landscape. First, they depict characteristically vivid and powerful scenes of specific moments in our lives. Whether it's the process of laboring, traces of his own family history, or moments of observing neighbors, his poems originate from the depth of the Korean language, embracing veracity and sincerity. In this sense, they continue the tradition of depicting experiences and observations of marginalized labor and of recovering the lives of people who have experienced and endured the times of such work, as captured by poets from Shin Kyeong-nim to Kim Sin-yong; yet they also contain more-diverse details than poems by his predecessors. Second, his poems are characterized by an exceptional undercurrent: a sense of rhythm that considers the readers' breaths. Through his highly personal poetic rhythms, sometimes passionately and other times placidly, he evokes such varied feelings as anger, withdrawal, sympathy, and love in a remarkably heartfelt language. This is an aesthetic achievement of Kim Myoung Ki's poetry that will continue to amaze the Korean world of poetry. Third, his poems are highly lyrical, and, in addition, the objects of Kim's lyricism are not just entities like people, moments, and scenes, but also more comprehensive and abstract values, like hope, the future, and life. These three characteristics of Kim's poetry form a beautiful triangle and make his poems stand out.

After living away from his home village for a long time, Kim Myoung Ki returned in early winter 12 years ago to attend his father's funeral, and has been living there since with his elderly mother, while writing poems about life in this remote place, where traces of human life are becoming sparser. Sometimes he sings about the difficulties and precariousness of lives "like residual images growing as time goes by" ("Heartbroken in Spring"), and, at other times, about hopes "like ice cubes" that are "sparkling" and “melting” inside “the coffee as dark as the phrase ‘temporary worker’” (“Future Without a Future”).

Although I am reminded of the heartless summer days of
Surrenders older than me, who will someday no longer be in this world,
Like the light-brown iced americanos showing their bottoms, in order to shut my mouth,
Unable to talk about them, chewing lingering ice cubes until my teeth freeze,
I think of the future, when even that temporarily heroic past will no longer be.
—From “Future Without a Future”

Kim could anticipate "the future when even that temporarily heroic past would no longer be" only because his poems originate from the marginality of the lives depicted in them. He records the time of "quietly pushing away sadness," ("While Quietly Pushing Away Sadness"), or confesses that he "avoid[s] that hilltop, where there is no longer any trace of human presence" on his way home, because he feels "as if [he] turned away from the moment that [he] did not know,/The moment when [the man] might have been living fully, no matter how paltry a life" ("Corpse"). About a "man sending incantations on a wind for days/After hanging a tattered bedsheet near the sea," he sees "the ardent desires... which seeped out of our bones" when "we desperately miss someone whom we can see never again,/Or when it seems that the whole world is collapsing, as we scold ourselves/For being careless, as our lives seem to touch the polar region" ("White-Haired Madman"). When Kim asks, "What could be more miserable/Than the pitiable that cannot be condemned?" ("Discarding Shoes"), his version of apocalypse appears sometimes as himself "fallen asleep after yearning for sadness that did not brush against me or that simply passed me by" ("Monsoon") or accepting that "For a life to set is to become gentler,/After tenaciously enduring and withstanding" ("Cutting a Donarium Cherry").

And a man with a bloody bandage around his
    head, over the ruins,
Toward God's grace gotten lost on its way,
Kneels down and slowly raises his arms.

—From "Evening News"

People who are closest to despair,
People who fill spaces left empty by death, just to
eat,
Death by being trapped, death by falling, death by
being dragged, death while walking.

The last and tiniest component of evolving
capitalism that degrades
Workers: their hourly wage as their class, as they
move from one bottom
To another, while ever lowering their bodies behind
unfamiliar desires and betrayed expectations—
—From "Precariat"

About the recent events in which Israeli attacks

on Gaza have resulted in enormous casualties, including the death of premature babies in incubators, he testifies, "over the ruins, as if to hasten death,/Flares flash." He depicts the shade of history where "a man with a bloody bandage around his head" helplessly clashes with "God's grace gotten lost on its way." He also condemns the despair in the reality of contemporary labor in which the dying fill the empty spaces left by deaths, just to eat. When he summons "[w] orkers for whom their hourly wage is their class, as they move from one bottom/To another," Kim's observations and poetic touch are both fierce and sorrowful. These subjects and expressions testify to the scale and timeliness of Kim's poems.

Like names that have undergone the colonial
    period and endless ideological strife,
An angular and steep land with which I know
    neither what to do
Nor how long it was unused—
I became its landlord.
—From "Landlord"

To rent a room at a damp place where the ocean
    fog
Seeps under the floor paper in early morning is to
    briefly lay an empty body
So that it might communicate with black fungi.
    For a person who can get up and leave anytime
For the work of living, his body is the bedding,
    furniture, and dishes....
While I am thinking of these things,
A person who hasn't yet arrived at the swinging

sign
Might be managing to drag his body, his only
possession,
And pass a point in this world like an exile.
—From "While I Am Thinking Of These Things"

The territory of Kim's poems also embraces stories of previous generations of his family, who have been living and enduring through the Japanese colonial period and the era of division on the Korean peninsula. Through the process of becoming the landlord of an old piece of land, out of the blue, he shows the context in which "names that have undergone the colonial period and endless ideological strife" are still to be summoned. About anybody "who can get up and leave anytime/For the work of living" and for whom "his body is the bedding, furniture, and dishes," he thinks of how he "[m]ight be managing to drag his body, his only possession,/ And pass a point in this world like exile." Yet, as these experiences and thoughts do not drive Kim only into deep depression and pessimism, we notice a sense of balance and paradoxical hope in his poems.

> The night of destruction that is irredeemable
> Will come like that, burying greed that does not
>   know humiliation
> And eternal sadness into a bottomless pit,
> Like the desperate voice of an old singer who does
>   not sing about the future.
> —From "At Night, Listening to Night of
>   Destruction"

In the early spring, a forest fire erupted. For 11
days
Even forests faraway burned to the ground. After
the trees had burned, though,
The mountains remained as they were, but like
blackened furnaces.
Water deer, racoons, and wild pigs, avoiding the
fire,
Ran down even to the main street. But as they had
nowhere else to go,
They reluctantly returned to the charred remains of
the mountain forests.
Humans who had lost their houses to the fire, like
the helpless
Mountain animals, also had nowhere else to go,
So they brought containers like huts to live in
At the foothills of the mountains.

—"The Work of Living" (the entire poem)

At night when he is listening to Hahn Daesoo's "Night of Destruction," Kim emphasizes that he would sing in a "desperate voice" while "burying greed that does not know humiliation/ And eternal sadness into a bottomless pit," even if the "night of destruction that is irredeemable" would come. Singing and listening to a song like that, we will continue to live even when "forests faraway burned to the ground" due to a forest fire. People who "had lost their houses to the fire" will also continue to live at the foothills of those mountains. "The work of living" is sorrowful and painful but it will continue.

To read Kim Myoung Ki's poems is a process accompanied by pain and fascination. While dealing with the contemporary lives of marginalized outsiders, his poems testify to why theirs are so difficult. Thus, they appear as a poetics of tragedy, as tragedy is what we feel when the good and beautiful are defeated in the world. Although the good and beautiful get erased, decay, and are often defeated within the mainstream order in Kim's poems, they are yet proven to be supporters of this world. That is why they present to us complete and precious testimonies of our times and hopes like sparkling, melting ice cubes.

PRAISES FOR KIM MYOUNG KI

Kim Myoung Ki's poems are different from a group of compositions that have a 'broken mirror' as their subjects. They are also different from lighter ecological poems that consider nature as superior to humans and urge humans to reflect on themselves. Nor are they similar to old-fashioned lyrical poems that contain yearnings or loneliness in the center of concentric circles. I am not arguing that his poems are entirely different and new. They are connected to the genealogy of *minjung* or labor literature of a generation ago. Yet they not only continue the tradition, but also establish their own new world. Perhaps we can call them the lyrical manifestations of a social self, or the social manifestation of a lyrical self. Thus, they get angry but aren't swayed by emotions, they reproach themselves but don't despair, they sympathize but do not pity, and they are hopeful, but not overly excited. They are the language of sincerity that can come only from a person who has undergone twists and turns as well as the bitter anxieties and pains of life.

—from Lee Moon-jae (poet),
Judges' Remarks for the 22nd Gosan
Literature Grand Prize

There are many people who are bearing invisible yet heavy burdens in this world. Occasionally, their invisible burdens are found out by others unintentionally. Contrastingly, we sometimes recognize their heavy burdens on our own. When burdens recognize burdens, they lean on each other and share the difficulty. Although the sum of the burden does not decrease, our steps become a little bit lighter. Poet Kim Myoung Ki describes it as: "Sadness recognizes sadness." He also says, "Sadness can be endured only when we are all sad together." These words are sincere and true. To sadness, sadness, to pain, pain is a friend, a neighbor, and a shelter.

—from Na Min-ae (literary critic),
"Na Min-ae's Life Penetrated by Poetry"

K-POET

At Night, Listening to Night of Destruction

Written by Kim Myoung Ki
Translated by Jeon Seung-hee
Published by ASIA Publishers
Address 445, Hoedong-gil, Paju-si, Gyeonggi-do, Korea
(Seoul Office: 161-1, Seodal-ro, Dongjak-gu,Seoul, Korea)
Email bookasia@hanmail.net
ISBN 979-11-5662-317-5 (set) | 979-11-5662-712-8 (04810)
First published in Korea by ASIA Publishers 2024

*This book is published with the support of the Literature Translation Institute of Korea (LTI Korea).

K-픽션 시리즈 | Korean Fiction Series

〈K-픽션〉 시리즈는 한국문학의 젊은 상상력입니다. 최근 발표된 가장 우수하고 흥미로운 작품을 엄선하여 출간하는 〈K-픽션〉은 한국문학의 생생한 현장을 국내외 독자들과 실시간으로 공유하고자 기획되었습니다. 〈바이링궐 에디션 한국 대표 소설〉 시리즈를 통해 검증된 탁월한 번역진이 참여하여 원작의 재미와 품격을 최대한 살린 〈K-픽션〉 시리즈는 매 계절마다 새로운 작품을 선보입니다.

001 버핏과의 저녁 식사-**박민규** Dinner with Buffett-**Park Min-gyu**
002 아르판-**박형서** Arpan-**Park hyoung su**
003 애드벌룬-**손보미** Hot Air Balloon-**Son Bo-mi**
004 나의 클린트 이스트우드-**오한기** My Clint Eastwood-**Oh Han-ki**
005 이베리아의 전갈-**최민우** Dishonored-**Choi Min-woo**
006 양의 미래-**황정은** Kong's Garden-**Hwang Jung-eun**
007 대니-**윤이형** Danny-**Yun I-hyeong**
008 퇴근-**천명관** Homecoming-**Cheon Myeong-kwan**
009 옥화-**금희** Ok-hwa-**Geum Hee**
010 시차-**백수린** Time Difference-**Baik Sou linne**
011 올드 맨 리버-**이장욱** Old Man River-**Lee Jang-wook**
012 권순찬과 착한 사람들-**이기호** Kwon Sun-chan and Nice People-**Lee Ki-ho**
013 알바생 자르기-**장강명** Fired-**Chang Kang-myoung**
014 어디로 가고 싶으신가요-**김애란** Where Would You Like To Go?-**Kim Ae-ran**
015 세상에서 가장 비싼 소설-**김민정** The World's Most Expensive Novel-**Kim Min-jung**
016 체스의 모든 것-**김금희** Everything About Chess-**Kim Keum-hee**
017 할로윈-**정한아** Halloween-**Chung Han-ah**
018 그 여름-**최은영** The Summer-**Choi Eunyoung**
019 어느 피씨주의자의 종생기-**구병모** The Story of P.C.-**Gu Byeong-mo**
020 모르는 영역-**권여선** An Unknown Realm-**Kwon Yeo-sun**
021 4월의 눈-**손원평** April Snow-**Sohn Won-pyung**
022 서우-**강화길** Seo-u-**Kang Hwa-gil**
023 가출-**조남주** Run Away-**Cho Nam-joo**
024 연애의 감정학-**백영옥** How to Break Up Like a Winner-**Baek Young-ok**
025 창모-**우다영** Chang-mo-**Woo Da-young**
026 검은 방-**정지아** The Black Room-**Jeong Ji-a**
027 도쿄의 마야-**장류진** Maya in Tokyo-**Jang Ryu-jin**
028 홀리데이 홈-**편혜영** Holiday Home-**Pyun Hye-young**
029 해피 투게더-**서장원** Happy Together-**Seo Jang-won**
030 골드러시-**서수진** Gold Rush-**Seo Su-jin**
031 당신이 보고 싶어하는 세상-**장강명** The World You Want to See-**Chang Kang-myoung**
032 지난밤 내 꿈에-**정한아** Last Night, In My Dream-**Chung Han-ah**
Special 휴가중인 시체-**김중혁** Corpse on Vacation-**Kim Jung-hyuk**
Special 사파에서-**방현석** Love in Sa Pa-**Bang Hyeon-seok**